MANNERS ALWAYS MATTER

Illustrated by Lance Raichert
Written by Caleb Burroughs

7373 North Cicero Avenue, Lincolnwood, Illinois 60712
Ground Floor, 59 Gloucester Place, London W1U 8JJ
www.pilbooks.com

Manufactured in China.
ISBN 1-4127-3009-0

Puppy was sad. He had broken his leg when he fell off of his bike.

Now his leg really hurt. It was in a big, itchy cast. He couldn't even walk around without using a pair of crutches.

There would be no running and playing for Puppy for quite a while. At least not until his leg had completely healed.

"Oh, no," said Puppy as he tried to make it to the bus stop. "It's really hard to walk with crutches."

He had to carry his heavy backpack full of books, his sack lunch, two crutches, and that big, heavy, itchy cast.

And he had to make it to the bus on time, too!

When the bus picked Puppy up, he was glad that his friends were there to help.

"I'll carry your lunch," said Mouse. "And I can hold onto your crutches."

"I'll zip up your backpack for you," offered Piggy.

"Thank you," said Puppy. But he was still awful sad about his broken leg.

With the help of his friends, Puppy got to school just fine.

But he still wasn't very good at walking with crutches.

"Whoa!" cried Puppy, as he tripped and stumbled. His good friends Bunny and Turtle held onto him.

"Thank you, Bunny and Turtle," said Puppy. "I would've fallen if you hadn't helped me."

At recess, Puppy felt especially sad and lonely. He watched as his friends ran and played catch.

"What's the matter, Puppy?" asked Mrs. Hen. "Why the long face?"

"Oh, Mrs. Hen," said Puppy. "With this crummy broken leg, I can't play with my friends."

"Well, I might have just the idea for you," said Mrs. Hen.

"Mrs. Hen said you were blue because you can't play at recess," said Mouse.

"So we decided to set up a game that you *can* play — a board game!" said Kitty.

"Thank you," said Puppy. "Even if I can't run and jump right now, I can still play games with my friends."

After recess, Puppy's friends had another surprise for him.

Dipping their paws in paint, each friend signed the cast. First Bear did. Then Kitty did. Finally, little Mouse placed a red paw-print on the bottom of the cast.

"Wow!" said Puppy. "Now my cast is really special. Thank you!"

Once Puppy's cast came off, he could run and jump. He didn't forget to thank his friends for all of their help.

Thank You

When someone helps you or does something nice, always remember to say "thank you."